A Kiss Like This

Catherine &
Laurence Anholt

TED SMART

When Little Cub was born,
Big Golden Lion just
couldn't stop kissing him.

"GRRRR!" he growled. "You're the most kissable cub in the world."

Big Golden Lion kissed Little Cub behind
his prickly ears . . . *just like this.*

And Little Cub giggled.

He kissed Little Cub on the end of his
small pink nose . . . *just like this.*

And Little Cub wriggled.

He kissed Little Cub right on his warm fat tummy and blew a raspberry on his belly button . . .

just like this.

And Little Cub giggled and wriggled and jiggled.

In the golden evening
sunshine, Little Cub played outside.

Everyone who passed by and saw Little Cub
wanted to kiss him too.

They just couldn't help it.

Along came Jumpy Monkey

and gave Little Cub a tickly
monkey kiss behind his
prickly ears,

on the end of his small pink nose

and right in the middle of his warm fat tummy . . .

just like this.

And Little Cub giggled and wriggled and jiggled.

Along came Squawky Parrot

and gave Little Cub a pecky
parrot kiss behind his
prickly ears,

on the end of his
small pink nose

and right in the middle of his warm fat tummy . . .

just like this.

And Little Cub giggled and wriggled and jiggled even more.

Along came
Big Fat Rhino

and gave Little Cub a
nuzzling nosy rhino
kiss behind his
prickly ears,

on the end of his
small pink nose

and right in the middle of his warm fat
tummy . . .

just like this.

And Little Cub giggled and wriggled and
jiggled all over again.

Along came Slippery Snake

and gave Little Cub a
s-s-slow hiss-s-sing
s-s-snake kiss-s-s
behind his prickly
ears-s-s,

on the end of his
small pink nos-s-se

and right in the middle of his warm fat
tummy . . .

just like this-s-s.

And Little Cub giggled and wriggled and
jiggled even more still.

Along came
Old Grey Elephant

and gave Little Cub a
slurpy sloppy elephant
kiss behind his
prickly ears,

on the end of his
small pink nose

and right in the middle of his warm fat tummy . . .

just like this.

And Little Cub giggled and wriggled and jiggled more than ever.

Then, last of all, along came
Mean Green Hungry Crocodile
snapping his wicked white teeth.

He saw Little Cub
playing in the
golden evening
sunshine.

"Little Cub, you certainly
are the most kissable cub
in the world.

"Come over here and I will give you a
snippy snappy crocodile kiss."

But Little Cub didn't want a snippy snappy
crocodile kiss at all. And he began to cry.

Mean Green Hungry Crocodile opened
his mean green hungry mouth and showed
all his wicked white crocodile teeth . . .

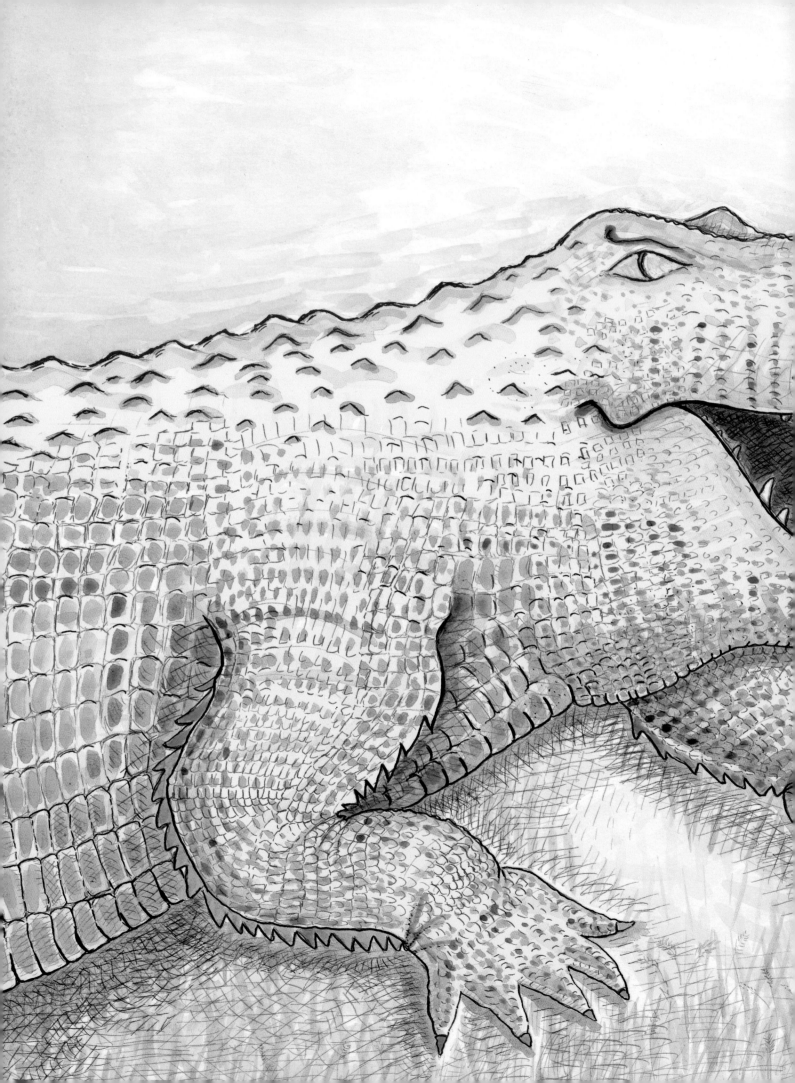

JUST
LIKE
THIS!

Quick as a flash, along came Big Golden
Lion and **ROARED** a Big
Golden Lion **ROAR** until Mean Green
Hungry Crocodile turned and ran away.

Big Golden Lion carried Little Cub back to their safe warm home and tucked him into his safe warm bed.

Then Big Golden Lion
stretched himself. "Listen,
Little Cub," he said.

"There's nothing better
than a tickly monkey kiss –
when you're a tiny monkey.

"And a parrot peck is
perfect – when you're
a baby parrot.

"No one loves a rhino
nuzzle quite like a
newborn rhino.

"A s-s-snake kiss-s-s is especially nic-c-ce – when you're a baby snake.

"And you can't have too many elephant kisses – when you're a little elephant.

"And *even* snippy snappy baby crocodiles love snippy snappy kisses."

"But", said Big Golden Lion, yawning, "when you're a sleepy Little Lion Cub, there's only one thing in the whole wide world that's completely, exactly right . . .

"And that's . . ."

A **HUGE GREAT**
Big Golden Lion kiss . . .

just like this!

For Jill Anholt
with a kiss like this

HAMISH HAMILTON LTD

Published by the Penguin Group
Penguin Books Ltd, 27 Wrights Lane, London W8 5TZ, England
Penguin Putnam Inc., 375 Hudson Street, New York, New York 10014, USA
Penguin Books Australia Ltd, Ringwood, Victoria, Australia
Penguin Books Canada Ltd, 10 Alcorn Avenue, Toronto, Ontario, Canada M4V 3B2
Penguin Books (NZ) Ltd, 182–190 Wairau Road, Auckland 10, New Zealand

Penguin Books Ltd, Registered Offices: Harmondsworth, Middlesex, England

First published 1997
3 5 7 9 10 8 6 4 2

Text copyright © Laurence Anholt, 1997
Illustrations copyright © Catherine Anholt, 1997

The moral right of the author and illustrator has been asserted

Filmset in Bembo

Made and printed in Singapore by Imago

British Library Cataloguing in Publication Data
A CIP catalogue record for this book is available from the British Library

ISBN 0–241–13693–8

This edition produced for
The Book People, Hall Wood Avenue, Haydock, St Helens, WA11 9UL